ISBN 0 86112 766 8
Published by Brimax Books Ltd, Newmarket, England. 1991.
Second printing 1992.
Printed in Hong Kong.

My First
Christmas
Storybook

ILLUSTRATED BY GILL GUILE

Brimax Books · Newmarket · England

The Night Before Christmas

'Twas the night before Christmas,
When all through the house
Not a creature was stirring,
Not even a mouse;
The stockings were hung
By the chimney with care,
In hopes that St Nicholas
Soon would be there;
The children were nestled
All snug in their beds,
While visions of sugar plums
Danced in their heads.

And Mamma in her 'kerchief,
And I in my cap,
Had just settled our brains
For a long winter's nap,
When out on the lawn
There arose such a clatter,
I sprang from the bed
To see what was the matter.
Away to the window
I flew like a flash,
Tore open the shutters
And threw up the sash.

The moon, on the breast
Of the new fallen snow,
Gave the lustre of mid-day
To objects below,
When what to my wondering
Eyes should appear,
But a miniature sleigh,
And eight tiny reindeer,
With a little old driver,
So lively and quick,
I knew in a moment
It must be St Nick.

More rapid than eagles
His coursers they came,
And he whistled and shouted,
And called them by name;
"Now, Dasher! Now, Dancer!
Now, Prancer and Vixen!
On, Comet! On, Cupid!
On, Donner and Blitzen
To the top of the porch!
To the top of the wall!
Now, dash away! Dash away!
Dash away all!"

As dry leaves that before
The wild hurricane fly,
When they meet with an obstacle,
Mount to the sky;
So up to the housetop
The coursers they flew,
With the sleigh full of toys,
And St Nicholas too.

And then, in a twinkling,
I heard on the roof
The prancing and pawing
Of each little hoof –
As I drew in my head,
And was turning around,
Down the chimney St Nicholas
Came with a bound.

He was dressed all in fur,
From his head to his foot,
And his clothes were all tarnished
With ashes and soot;
A bundle of toys he had
Flung on his back,
And he looked like a pedlar
Just opening his pack.
His eyes – how they twinkled!
His dimples, how merry!
His cheeks were like roses,
His nose like a cherry.

His droll little mouth
Was drawn up like a bow,
And the beard of his chin
Was as white as the snow;
The stump of his pipe he held
Tight in his teeth,
And the smoke it encircled
His head like a wreath;
He had a broad face
And a little round belly
That shook, when he laughed,
Like a bowlful of jelly.

He was chubby and plump,
A right jolly old elf,
And I laughed, when I saw him,
In spite of myself;
A wink of his eye
And a twist of his head,
Soon gave me to know
I had nothing to dread;
He spoke not a word,
But went straight to his work,
And filled all the stockings;
Then turned with a jerk,

And laying his finger
Aside of his nose,
And giving a nod,
Up the chimney he rose;
He sprang to his sleigh,
To his team gave a whistle,
And away they all flew
Like the down of a thistle.
But I heard him exclaim,
Ere he drove out of sight,
"Happy Christmas to all,
And to all a good night."

Clement C Moore

Jingle bells! Jingle bells!
Jingle all the way,
Oh, what fun it is to ride
In a one-horse open sleigh.

Dashing through the snow,
In a one-horse open sleigh,
Merrily we go,
Laughing all the way.

Bells on bob-sleigh ring,
Making spirits bright,
Oh, what fun it is to ride
In a one-horse sleigh tonight.

Jingle bells! Jingle bells!
Jingle all the way,
Oh, what fun it is to ride
In a one-horse open sleigh.

Traditional

Say these words again.

moon	snow
chimney	plump
window	reindeer
whistled	house
sleigh	soot
roof	teeth
bundle	twinkled

What can you see?

sleigh

reindeer

stocking

toys

Christmas tree

Santa
Claus

Santa Claus was polishing his big, black boots. They were so shiny he could see his own smiling face in them.

"I must look my best on Christmas Eve," said Santa. "Even if I am covered in soot by Christmas morning." He pulled on his boots and his red jacket.

"Ready to go!" said Santa.

Mr Holly was Santa's helper.
He was tall and thin and wore
a suit made of holly leaves.
Mr Holly was looking for his hat.
Where could it be? He picked up
Snowflake the cat. There was
his hat! He brushed it quickly
and put it on.
"Ready to go!" said Mr Holly.

Outside, the reindeer were tossing their heads and stamping their feet.
They couldn't wait to be off! This was the most exciting night of the year. Santa Claus and Mr Holly began to load the sleigh with toys and games. Soon the sleigh was stacked high.
"Ready to go!" said everyone.

Mr Holly sat next to Santa and looked at the map. At last Santa flicked the reins and the sleigh lifted into the night. There was a full moon and the stars twinkled brightly in the sky. "A perfect Christmas Eve," said Santa Claus. The reindeer nodded and the sleigh bells jingled in the frosty air.

Soon they reached the first house. Santa Claus climbed down the chimney. He read the list pinned to a stocking by the fireplace.

"Mandy would like a teddy and a clock," called Santa up the chimney. Mr Holly searched in the sacks and found the right presents. He handed them down to Santa, who put them in the stocking.

When Santa Claus climbed down Ben's chimney, he fell into an enormous sack stretched across the fireplace. "Oh, my boots and whiskers!" said Santa in surprise. He scrambled out, tangled up in the longest list he had ever seen. "What a greedy boy," said Santa. "If I give him all these presents, some children will have none."

"Pass the sack up to me," said Mr Holly, then he found a sewing box and set to work with needle and cotton. Snip, snip, snip went the scissors. In and out went the needle. At last Mr Holly held up a tiny stocking cut out of the enormous sack. "This should be big enough for just one present," he said.

Then the sleigh landed on the roof of a little crooked cottage. The door twisted one way, the window twisted the other. Even the chimney was twisted, just like a corkscrew. Santa Claus took a deep breath and started to climb down. But at the first twist he got stuck.

"Help! Help!" cried Santa.

Mr Holly tugged. The reindeer
tugged. At last Santa popped
out of the chimney.
"What shall we do?" he asked.
Mr Holly took a fishing rod
from the back of the sleigh. He
dropped the line down the
chimney, then pulled up a
yellow stocking.
"Paul would like a watch,"
said Mr Holly.
Santa filled the stocking and
lowered it down the chimney.

They travelled through the night, climbing down chimneys and filling stockings until they came to the last house. Santa found a pair of purple stockings which belonged to Tessa and Tom, who were twins. Mr Holly searched among the sacks. "Santa Claus," called Mr Holly down the chimney, "I am afraid there are no more presents!"

Santa searched the sacks, too. "This has never happened to me before," he said. "Santa Claus can't run out of presents! Whatever shall we do, Mr Holly? Tessa and Tom will wake up to find empty stockings." Santa and Mr Holly sat side by side on the roof and thought and thought.

"What would the twins like for Christmas?" asked Mr Holly. Santa read the list then he clapped his hands in delight. "Of course! Read this, Mr Holly." Mr Holly put on his glasses. "Dear Santa Claus," he read, "our Dad is the local toymaker so we don't need any toys. Could we have a sleigh ride instead, please? From Tessa and Tom."

How Tessa and Tom enjoyed their sleigh ride. They took turns to hold the reins and drove round the town three times. They could see their friends' houses and Grandma's cottage by the lake. At last they landed on their own roof. The twins waved goodbye and jingled the sleigh bells Santa had given them. They would remember this perfect Christmas Eve forever!

Say these words again.

polishing	cottage
buttons	watch
exciting	searched
frosty	delight
clock	forever
enormous	shiny
present	reins

What can you see?

boots

teddy

fishing rod

cat

sleigh bells

Snow for Christmas

"Will it snow this Christmas?"
Polly asked her mother.
"I've never seen snow,"
said Sam. "Except in pictures."
"We'll have to wait and see if
Mother Goose shakes her
feathers," said his mother.
"That's what my Grandma used
to say to me when it snowed –
Mother Goose is shaking her
feathers again."
"That's silly," said Sam.
Mother smiled. "Is it?"

On Christmas Eve, Polly and Sam went to bed early. They hung their stockings up ready for Santa Claus. Soon they were fast asleep. Suddenly, Polly woke up. "Sam! I can hear a noise!" She crept to the window, lifted the curtain and peeped out into the darkness.

Polly could hardly believe her eyes. Outside was a goose. Not an ordinary goose like the ones in Farmer Smith's field, this goose wore a green bonnet and a red shawl. She was searching for something in the bushes. "Wake up, Sam!" cried Polly. Sam stirred and opened one eye. "It's Mother Goose," said Polly.

"Don't be silly," grumbled
Sam. "That was just a story.
You've been dreaming."
"No I have not!" said Polly.
"She's out there and she looks
exactly like Mother Goose in
my storybook."
"I suppose she's carrying
a sack of feathers to shake
over us," said Sam with a yawn.
But he still went to the window
to have a look.

"Whatever shall I do?" Mother Goose was saying. "Where can it be?" She lifted the lid of the rain barrel and looked inside. "I'm sure I left it here. There'll be no snow for Christmas now." Polly opened the bedroom window and called, "Can we help, Mother Goose?"

The sound of Polly's voice above her head made Mother Goose squawk in alarm. "How you startled me! I've lost my sack of feathers," she explained. "I must find it or there'll be no snow for Christmas." Polly and Sam quickly dressed and ran downstairs to help Mother Goose in her search.

Polly searched in the woodshed. She found sacks of logs and long-legged spiders. Sam searched in the greenhouse. He found sacks of potatoes and dusty flowerpots. Mother Goose searched in the barn. She found sacks of corn and squeaking mice. Nobody found a sack of feathers.

"When did you last have your sack?" asked Sam.

"Yesterday," said Mother Goose, "when I passed your house. I stopped to talk to a friend. Then I went on, leaving the feathers behind."

"Someone else must have found it," said Polly. "There are only two houses along this road. Ours and Mrs Crackle's."

"Let's ask Mrs Crackle," said Sam.

They found Mrs Crackle sitting beside a blazing fire. "Come in," she said. "It's cold enough for snow."

"We shan't have any snow," said Sam.

"Not unless Mother Goose finds her sack of feathers," said Polly.

"Sack of feathers you say," said Mrs Crackle, beginning to smile. "I think I can help you."

Mrs Crackle led the way to a cupboard under the stairs. "The sack of feathers was by the road," she said. "No one came to collect it and the feathers were so clean and white, I decided to make myself a new feather quilt. But someone else had the same idea. Look!" Mrs Crackle shone a lamp into the dark cupboard.

There was Mother Goose's sack, and there was Mrs Crackle's ginger cat, Miranda, curled up in the soft feathers with five ginger kittens. "I can't disturb the kittens," said Mother Goose. "Don't worry," said Mrs Crackle. "We'll think of something."

Polly, Sam and Mother Goose
sat down to think. Before they
had even one idea, the door
opened and in padded
Miranda, carrying a kitten in
her mouth. She dropped him
gently on the hearth-rug.
Backwards and forwards she
went until all five kittens lay in
a furry heap, purring happily,
Miranda beside them.

Stopping only long enough to thank everyone and take her sack of feathers, Mother Goose flapped her wings and flew away. As Polly and Sam waved goodbye, a handful of soft, white feathers drifted down and the first snowflakes they had ever seen began to fall. "Snow for Christmas!" shouted Sam. "Thank you, Mother Goose!" said Polly.

Say these words again.

snow

bonnet

feathers

kitten

curtain

searching

yawn

lost

quickly

greenhouse

squeaking

barn

quilt

lamp

Who can you see?

Polly

Sam

Mother Goose

Mrs Crackle

Miranda

The First ⭐ Christmas

Long ago, in a town called Nazareth, there lived a young woman named Mary. One day a great light appeared and the angel Gabriel stood before her. "Do not be afraid," said the angel. "I bring you joyful news. God has chosen you to be the mother of his son. You will have a baby and you must call him Jesus."

In the same town there lived a carpenter named Joseph. Joseph loved Mary very much. He was going to marry her. The angel came to visit Joseph and told him that Mary was going to have God's son. Later Joseph came to see Mary and told her what the angel had said.

One day a message came from the governor of the land. All of the people had to go back to the place where they had been born so they could be counted. Joseph was worried. He and Mary would have to go to Bethlehem. This was a long way away and Mary was almost ready to have her baby.

They set off early the next morning. Joseph led the way. Mary rode on a donkey. The road was long and hard. They didn't reach Bethlehem until the evening. The town was full of people. Joseph tried everywhere to find a place to stay, but all the rooms were taken. Mary was so tired she could hardly stay awake.

At last an innkeeper said, "All my rooms are full, but you can use my stable. It is clean and warm in there."
Joseph thanked him and they went inside. All around them cows and donkeys lay peacefully asleep. The hay was soft and smelled sweet. Mary and Joseph lay down and rested.

In the night, Mary gave birth to her baby. It was a boy as the angel had said. They named him Jesus.
Mary wrapped him in a blanket and laid him in a manger, where it was soft and warm.
Mary and Joseph watched over Jesus lovingly. They knew he was a very special baby.

Out on the hillside above the town, some shepherds were looking after their sheep. Suddenly the sky was filled with light and an angel appeared. The shepherds fell to the ground in fear.

But the angel said, "Do not be afraid. I bring you good news. Today a child is born. He is the son of God. You will find him in Bethlehem, lying in a manger."

The shepherds gazed in wonder as the sky was filled with angels singing.

"We must go and find this child," said one. "We can take one of our newborn lambs as a gift."

They went to Bethlehem and found Jesus in the stable with Mary and Joseph. They fell to their knees and offered their gift.

Far away in an eastern land lived some wise men. One night they saw a bright new star in the sky. They wanted to know what it meant. They looked in their books for the answer. "It means that a new king has been born," they said. "We must go and look for him so that we can worship him. The star will guide us."

The wise men set off on their journey. The star shone brightly in front of them by day and by night. They came to the palace of King Herod who said to them, "You must find the new king then tell me where he is." King Herod was not very pleased.

The wise men followed
the star for many miles. It
stopped right over the stable
where Jesus lay. "We are
looking for the newborn king,"
they said. "A bright star has
guided us from far away."
Joseph led them into the
stable. They knelt before Jesus
and offered him some very
special gifts of gold,
frankincense and myrrh.

The next day, the wise men set out for King Herod's palace. They stopped to rest and while they were asleep an angel came to them in a dream. "Do not go back to Herod," the angel warned. "He does not want Jesus to be King." The wise men decided to go home a different way.

Mary and Joseph were very happy and proud. They knew their baby was really the son of God. They knew he was very special and that he would have important work to do when he grew up. They also knew that Jesus would be loved throughout the world and that people would remember his birth as a time of happiness and peace.

Say these words again.

carpenter	star
message	palace
donkey	special
stable	dream
blanket	happiness
sheep	bright
gift	worship

Who can you see?

Joseph

shepherd

Mary

Jesus

wise men